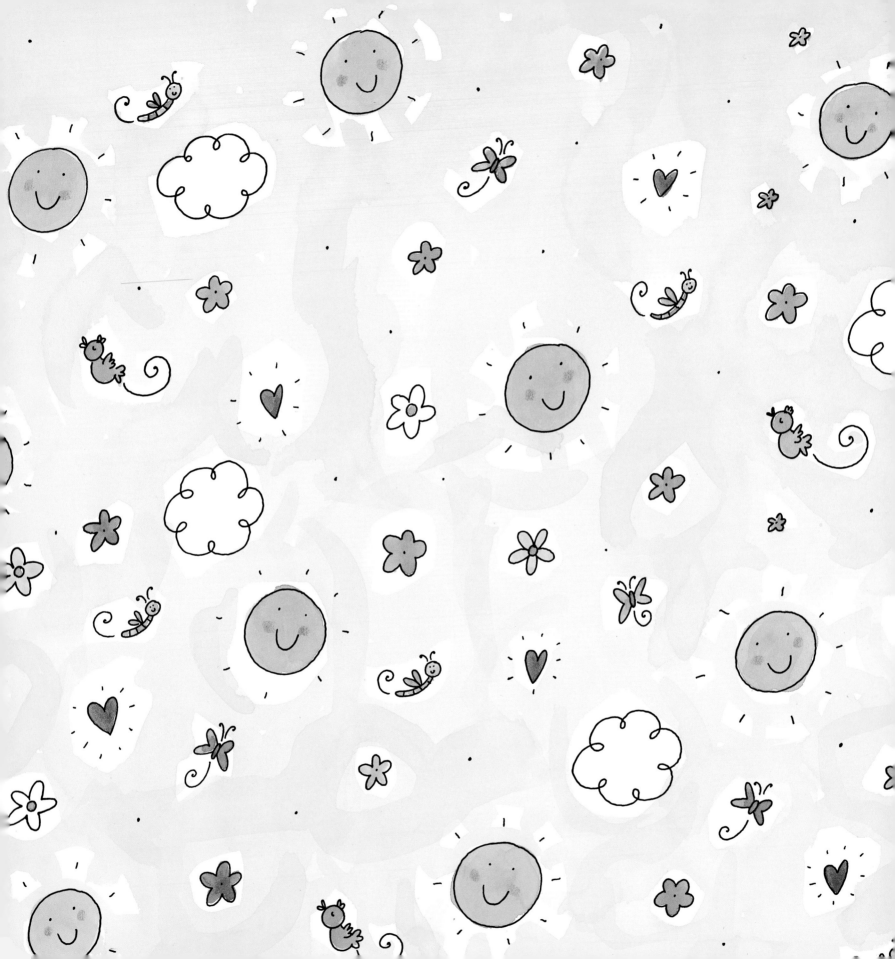

It's a Baby's World

by Amanda Haley

Little, Brown and Company
Boston   New York   London

sun

Good Morning, Baby!

butterflies

wake up with Mommy and Daddy

awake!

have a bottle

cup

toothpaste

toothbrush

watch the sunrise

diapers

get a diaper change

stuffed animal

ball

blanket

brush and comb

Getting Ready for the Day

spoon

pack the diaper bag

get dressed

eat breakfast

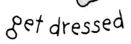

socks

T-shirt

juice

take off pajamas

diaper bag

drink milk

off to day care

bottle

feed the cat

cereal

Play Time

balloons

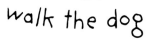
songbook

walk the dog

drive a car

keys

play in the playpen

draw

truck

airplane

rattle

make music

duck

paint

read a book

choo-choo train

crayons

blocks

dance

drum

Out and About

bugs

car

house

flower

go grocery shopping

visit the zoo

go for a walk

hug a dog

ride in a wagon

Lunch Time

sit in the high chair

share a cookie

messy baby

bananas

cherries

bowl

noodles

spoon

pizza

have a bottle

have a picnic

eat with a
spoon

grapes

eat a sandwich

apple

sit at the table

Nap Time

rock in a rocking chair

look at pictures

nap on a mat

count sheep

read a story

play with a mobile

sleep in a big bed

Baby Love

cuddle a
doll

Friends

hug a friend

play on the playground

seesaw

play with
a cat

kick a ball

go down the slide

dig in the sandbox

play with trains

Dinner

help cook

applesauce

eat dinner

glass

plate

set the table

take food out of the fridge

baby food

Family Time

play on the floor

friends and family

board game

read a book

swing on the porch

draw pictures

do a puzzle

puzzle

look at family photos

look at the stars

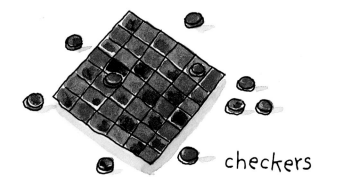

checkers

baby powder

Bath Time

wrap up in a towel

boat

play with bath toys

dry off

soap

splash in
the sink

pajamas

Good Night, Baby!

moon and stars

mobile

sing a lullaby

lamp

brush teeth

time for bed

bedtime book

night sky

soft music

peek-a-boo

read a story

go to sleep

pacifier

hug a blanket

bottle

To my husband, Brian,
for his love and patience.

First Edition

Library of Congress Cataloging-in-Publication Data
Haley, Amanda.
    It's a baby's world / by Amanda Haley — 1st ed.
        p. cm.
    Summary: Labeled pictures present familiar activities in the daily routine of
babies and toddlers.
    ISBN 0-316-34596-2
    [1. Babies — Fiction. 2. Toddlers — Fiction.] I. Title.
    PZ7.H13827 It 2001
    [E] — dc21   99-057102

                    10 9 8 7 6 5 4 3 2 1

                                TWP

                        Printed in Singapore

The illustrations for this book were done in watercolor and ink.
The text is set in Providence, and the display type is Fontesque.

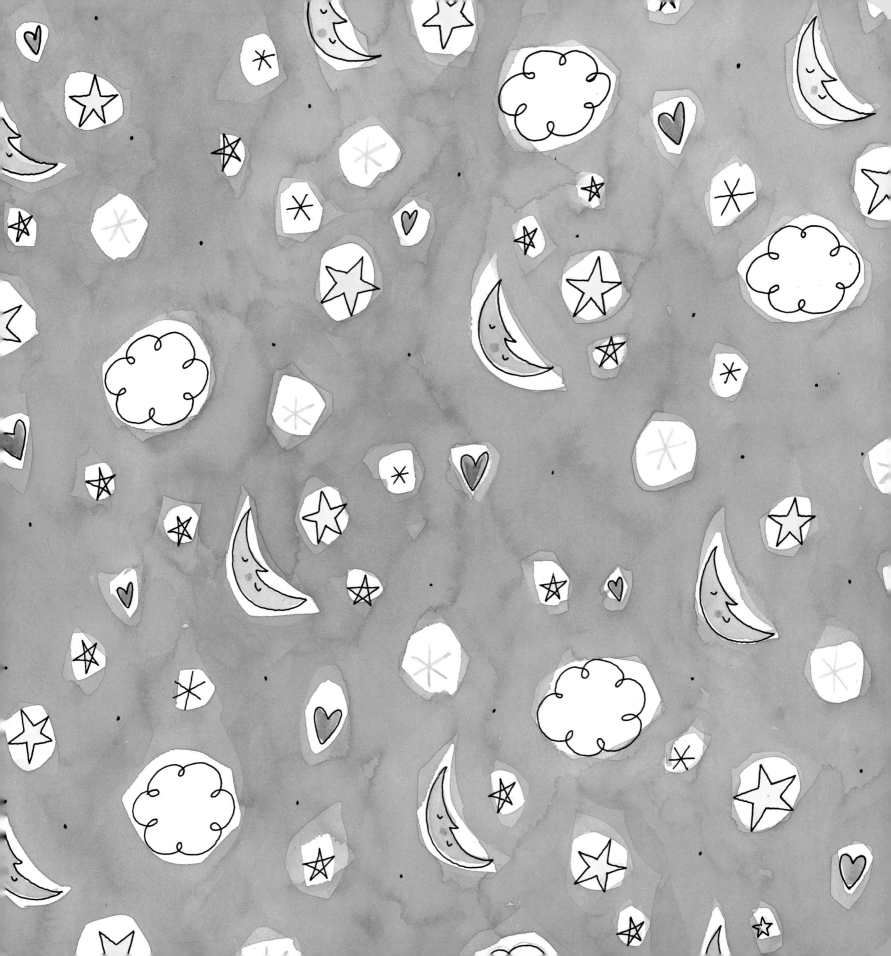

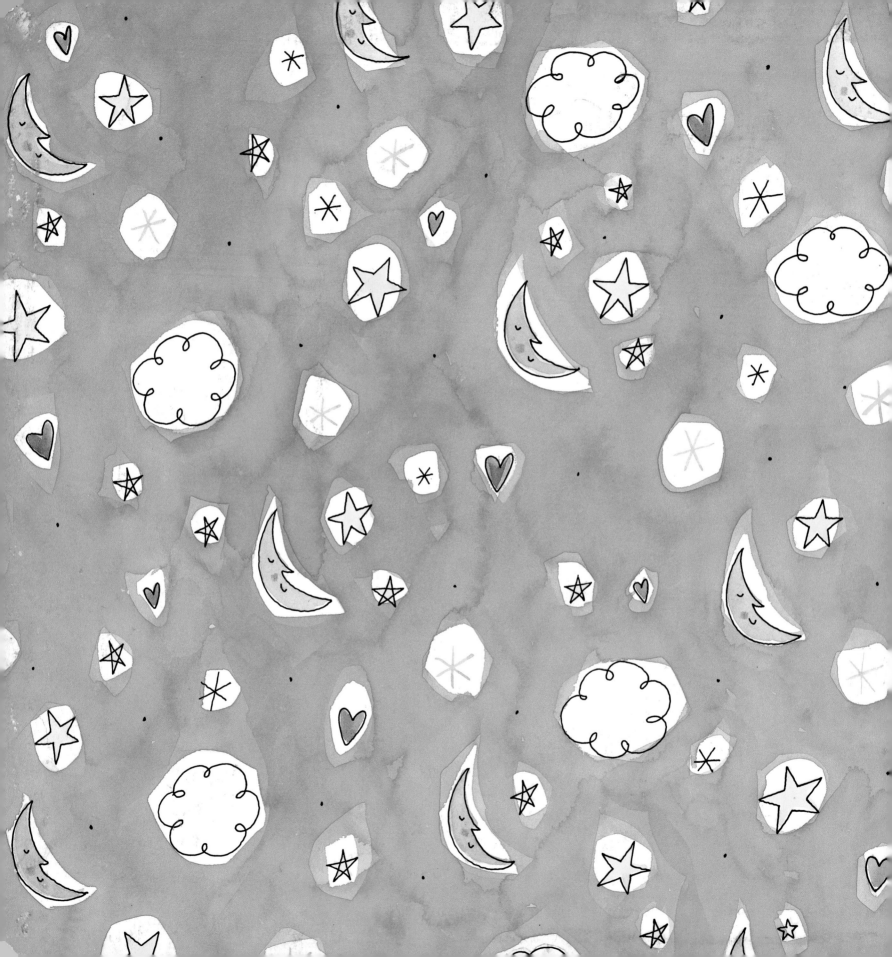